Caring

by Shelly Nielsen
illustrated by
Virginia Kylberg

Published by Abdo & Daughters, 6535 Cecilia Circle, Edina, Minnesota 55439

Copyright© 1992 by Abdo Consulting Group, Inc., Pentagon Tower, P.O. Box 36036, Minneapolis, Minnesota 55435. International copyrights reserved in all countries. No part of this book may be reproduced in any form without written permission from the publisher. Printed in the United States.

Edited by: Rosemary Wallner

Library of Congress Cataloging-in-Publication Data

Nielsen, Shelly, 1958-
    Caring / written by Shelly Nielsen ; edited by Rosemary Wallner.
       p. cm. -- (Values matter)
    Summary: Brief poems present portraits of children being caring and thoughtful to peers, adults, and animals.
    ISBN 1-56239-064-3
    1. Caring -- Juvenile poetry. 2. Children's poetry, American.
[1. Caring -- Poetry. 2. Conduct of life – Poetry. 3. American poetry.]
I. Wallner, Rosemary, 1964-   . II. Title. III. Series: Nielsen, Shelly, 1958- Values matter.
PS3564.I354C37 1992   811'.54--dc20   91-73044
                                                       CIP
                                                       AC

Caring

Abdo & Daughters
Minneapolis

I Am Here

Close your eyes, kitty,
I am here.
When I am beside you,
there's nothing to fear.
I'm watching and waiting,
softly petting your ears.
Close your eyes, kitty,
I am here.

Though the world
is big and wild,
though I'm just a little child,
I will hold you warm and near.
Close your eyes, kitty,
I am here.

Dear Pen Pal

Hello, pen pal,
far, far away.
I was thinking of you today.
So I'm sending this letter way over there
just to tell you:
I care!

I Care, They Care

I love Grandma and Grandpa;
they take good care of me.
When I want a bowl of popcorn,
they pop a batch or three.
When I get sleepy,
they tuck me into bed
and say, "We love you, honey."
Of course I care for them!

May I Help?

Look at me,
I'm big and strong.
My muscles grew
all summer long.
So let me carry that bag for you.
It's the very least
that I can do.

What Are Friends For?

Don't be sad, Tony,
we won't give up.
We'll find your marble
no matter what.
I'll check the sandbox,
you search the weeds.
I'll look in the flowers,
while you hunt under the tree.
Hey!
See what I found?
Something smooth, shiny, and round!

A New Friend

A little girl sat
all alone…
so I gave her a little smile.
"What's your name?
Want to join our game?"
Then she wasn't lonely for a while.

That Hurt!

Youch!   Ouch!
I fell off my bike!
Good thing Julie was there.
She brushed my knees
and smoothed my hair,
and said, "Are you all right?"
My arm was scratched,
my shorts were torn,
my bike was bent up, too.
But there's nothing better
for a fall off a bike
than a friend who cares for you.

Caring Cousin

My cousin Mandy is only three;
she follows me around and looks up to me.
I take her with me to the park
and hold her hand in the dark.
My cousin Mandy is only three;
I look after her; she looks up to me.

House Helper

I set the table--
Look at that!
Plate, fork, spoon, and place mat.
Won't Mom be happy
when she sees
what a big help I can be?

Don't Laugh

"Um...um..."
In the play
Hannah forgot
what she meant to say.
She stuttered
and stammered
and pretty soon
her face was red
as a balloon.
I wanted to laugh
but I kept my mouth closed.
Hannah already felt silly
from her hair to her toes.

Hello?

Ring-ring-ring.
I dialed up Aunt Lee
just to make her grin.
"That's funny," she said,
"I was just thinking of you,
and of all the sweet little
things that you do."

Favor For a Friend

Okay,
here we go.
Start at the top,
take it slow.
This strand.
That strand.
Start again.
I'm glad to braid the hair
of Kyra, my friend.

Paint Problems

When I helped Daddy
paint the wall,
the paint wouldn't stay put at all!
On my face,
in my hair,
purple paint,
everywhere.
But Daddy thanked me for helping out.
When you help your dad,
it's the thought that counts.